D1586627

NEWHAM LIBRARIES

90800101204380

PAW PATROL™

RESCUE Knights™

This storybook belongs to

....

First published in Great Britain in 2023 by Farshore
An imprint of HarperCollins*Publishers*
1 London Bridge Street, London SE1 9GF
www.farshore.co.uk

HarperCollins*Publishers*
Macken House, 39/40 Mayor Street Upper,
Dublin 1, D01 C9W8

©2023 Spin Master Ltd. ™PAW PATROL and all related titles, logos,
characters; and SPIN MASTER logo are trademarks of Spin Master Ltd.
Used under license. Nickelodeon and all related titles and logos are
trademarks of Viacom International Inc.

Illustrated by MJ Illustrations.

ISBN 978 0 0085 3405 9
Printed in the UK
001

A CIP catalogue record for this title is available from the British Library.

All rights reserved. No part of this publication may be reproduced, stored in a retrieval system,
or transmitted, in any form or by any means, electronic, mechanical, photocopying, recording
or otherwise, without the prior permission of the publisher and copyright owner.

Stay safe online. Farshore is not responsible for content hosted by third parties.

This book is produced from independently certified FSC™ paper
to ensure responsible forest management.

For more information visit: www.harpercollins.co.uk/green

DARING DRAGON RESCUE

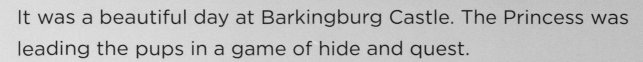

It was a beautiful day at Barkingburg Castle. The Princess was leading the pups in a game of hide and quest.

"I have to warn everyone," the Princess laughed, "I rule at hide and quest. Rescue Knights are you ready? Ten ... nine ... eight ..."

The pups all ran off to find the best hiding places. Marshall accidentally opened a secret tunnel and zoomed down into the castle gardens.

"Nice! The Princess will never find me out here," he chuckled.

Meanwhile, Sweetie was avoiding hide and quest, and taking a quiet walk in the forest.

"It's not fun when the Princess always wins," Sweetie complained to herself.

Up ahead she saw some baby dragons playing.

"Aw, baby dragons!" gasped Sweetie, in surprise. "They usually never leave the Dragon Highlands. I wonder what brought them here?"

Claw, a former Knight of Barkingburg and the Duke of Flappington, the Princess's mischievous cousin, were nearby. They were hatching a plan to take over the castle.

"The trick to trapping dragons is giving them something they love, like delicious marshmallows," whispered Claw.

They watched the baby dragons fly over to the Duke's wagon, following the delicious smell of the sweet marshmallows. The babies breathed their dragon fire, melting the tasty treats. They were too busy eating to notice the Duke and Claw hiding close by.

Sparks, Claw's pet dragon, smelled the yummy marshmallows too
and flew over to the wagon to eat some.

"Good trick," said the Duke, impressed.

"I happen to be very good at training dragons ..." said Claw, proudly.

He tip-toed over to the wagon and locked the baby dragons inside.

"... And catching them too," he said, as he attached the wagon to a
harness worn by Sparks.

"Now that I have a herd of dragons, I shall take over the castle and become King of Barkingburg!" smiled the Duke. "Now let me drive."

"Fine, but we'd better hope the fiery mother dragon doesn't find us." Claw said slyly. "I hear she has quite a temper."

"A d...dragon with a temper?" stuttered the Duke, "On second thoughts, Claw, you can drive. Bring me my dragon army when it's ready."

"Oh no!" exclaimed Sweetie, "The Duke and that naughty pup have taken those baby dragons! Their mama will be missing them! I'd better tell the Princess what they're up to." Sweetie rushed back to the castle to get help.

"Oh no, the poor little cuties," said Skye, once Sweetie had explained
what had happened.

"Their mama will be furious when she finds out they've been taken,"
said the Princess. "We must help them."

"Don't worry, your Highness," said Ryder. "No dragon is too angry; no
pup is too small. PAW Patrol to the Castle Lookout. Time for a daring
dragon rescue!"

The Rescue Knights assembled at the round table, ready for
Ryder's instructions.

"Chase, use your dragon megaphone and tell Claw to stop," Ryder said.

"Knight Chase is on the case," said Chase.

"Skye, I'll need you to put marshmallows on your grapples to lure the baby dragons off the wagon," Ryder continued.

"This puppy knight's gotta fly!" smiled Skye.

Chase, Ryder and Skye leaped into action.

The pups soon caught up with Claw, Sparks and the baby dragons.

"Let the dragons go, please," called Chase.

"No way," shouted Claw, "I caught 'em, I keep 'em."

"Who's hungry?" called Skye, as she lowered marshmallows on her grapple hooks. The baby dragons tried to jump free, but their feet were stuck to the sticky marshmallow!

Suddenly, the harness attached to Sparks broke and the wagon started to roll down the hill. Claw fell backwards into the sticky goo!

"Someone help me!" Claw shouted.

Ryder chased after the runaway wagon.

"Rescue Knights, I need you all for this rescue," he said.

"We're on our way, Sir Ryder," called Zuma. The rest of the PAW Patrol were ready to roll.

The wagon was rolling down the hill, heading towards some fallen trees. "Autopilot, dragon wings!" Skye said, swooping down to help. With only moments to spare, Skye told the stuck dragons to flap their wings, which lifted the wagon over the logs blocking its path.
The wagon soared through the air, landing on the other side with a bump, but it carried on rolling down the hill ...

All the noise attracted the attention of the mama dragon, who flew above, looking for her babies.

The PAW Patrol surrounded the wagon as it raced down the hill, now headed towards some rocks.

"Wrecking ball spinner on the double," said Rubble, as he smashed through the rocks, clearing a path for the runaway wagon.

Zuma activated his launcher and aimed three buoys at the wagon, making it swerve and slow to a stop at the edge of a high cliff.

The mama dragon glided down and landed in front of the wagon, roaring and stamping her feet in an effort to protect her babies. Her stomping shook the ground. Suddenly, CRACK! The cliff edge broke away, and the wagon slid over the edge!

"Rocky, use your talon hook to snag the wagon," called Ryder, quickly.

"I'm on it," said Rocky, as he hooked the falling wagon, slowly hoisting it back to safety.

"Help! I'm falling!" yelped Claw, as he slipped from the marshmallow goo.

"Activate dragon net," said Chase, releasing the net below the falling pup.

"Oooff," said Claw, landing safely. Claw's plans were defeated and he quietly sneaked away.

Once the babies were back on safe ground, Marshall got to work with his water jet.

"No more sticky marshmallow!" he winked, as he hosed the goo from the baby dragons' feet.

Finally free, the babies flew to Rocky and gave him a friendly lick to say thank you,
"Aw, you're welcome, little cuties," he laughed.

The baby dragons were finally reunited with their mama, who gave them a huge dragon hug! "Roooaaaar!" she said, happily.

"You're welcome, Mama Dragon," Ryder smiled. "Remember, whenever your babies are stuck in a marshmallowy mess, just roar for help."